A
BLIZZARD
YEAR

A BLiZZARD YEAR

TIMMY'S ALMANAC
of the
SEASONS

* * *

GRETEL EHRLICH

Illustrations by
KATE KIESLER

HYPERION BOOKS FOR CHILDREN

NEW YORK

Text copyright © 1999 by Gretel Ehrlich
Illustrations copyright © 1999 by Kate Kiesler
All rights reserved. No part of this book may be reproduced or transmitted in any
form or by any means, electronic or mechanical, including photocopying, recording,
or by any information storage and retrieval system, without written permission from
the publisher. For information address Hyperion Books for Children, 114 Fifth
Avenue, New York, New York 10011-5690.
First Edition
1 3 5 7 9 10 8 6 4 2
Printed in the United States of America.
Library of Congress Cataloging-in-Publication Data
Ehrlich, Gretel.
A blizzard year: Timmy's almanac of the seasons/Gretel Ehrlich;
illustrations by Kate Kiesler—1st ed.
p. cm.
Summary: For one year, thirteen-year-old Timmy records in her journal the changes
she sees in the natural world and her family's activities on their Wyoming ranch as
they fight to save it from financial ruin.
ISBN 0-7868-0364-9 (trade: alk.paper)—ISBN 0-7868-2309-7 (lib.: alk. paper)
[1. Ranch life—Wyoming—Fiction. 2. Seasons—Fiction. 3. Nature—Fiction.
4. Wyoming—Fiction. 5. Diaries—Fiction.] I. Kiesler, Kate, ill. II. Title.
PZ7.E333 Bl   1999
[Fic]—dc21   98-43730

For my Wyoming friends,
young and old,
human and animal.
And for Rhys Evans, godson, and Marie Louisa
and Itilik, Greenland-born.
Thanks to Timmy for lending me her name, and to
Leonard for lending me his house in Tuscarora.

✧ ✧ ✧

In memory of Michael Dorris,
Jenny Little,
and Gretchen, my mother.

FEBRUARY *is the month when you see a ring around the moon before a storm. It is always cold, sometimes twenty, thirty, or forty below zero. Snow is polished by wind, and the world looks smooth; trees are leafless skeletons that walk around the house at night and speak in a language that sounds like cracking bones. February is when the mother cows lie around on the snow and groan because soon they will be having calves. It is the month when ravens and horned owls mate, and deep inside*

grizzly and black bear dens, cubs are being born—hairless, sightless, and weighing only twelve to eighteen ounces. The mother bear nurses her cubs inside the den, never going out, never needing to eat, drink, or pee until the spring blizzards end.

* * *

February 10. Pedro shone the kerosene lamp on my face. "*Levántese, mi chula* . . . you have to get up now. . . . Okay?"

I looked out the tiny window. It was not quite light yet, but I could see that the narrow valley in front of Pedro's sheep wagon had been pillowed in deep snow during the night. The Dutch door was ajar—Pedro had gone outside. Fermina, his daughter—more or less—stood at the tiny cookstove. I say more or less because no one knows who her parents were. She was a foundling laid at Pedro's door. She is the closest thing I have to a sister.

I still remember the September day when Pedro came off the mountain with his band of sheep—a thousand animals—holding a small bundle in his arms. I had thought it was a newborn lamb. The long slopes were lion-colored with sun-cured grass, the robins were singing, and a few lazy eagles circled a meadow enclosed by pines. We were in the ranch truck at the bottom; we greeted him, looked inside the little bundle, and saw that it was a baby girl.

"I have called her Fermina, for my mother," he told my parents. My mother wanted to take care of the child, asking me if I would like a younger sister, but before I could answer yes, Pedro said no. He insisted on keeping her because, he said, an angel had sent this little girl to him and he must accept the gift. He would feed her ewe's milk from a bottle heated over the camp stove, just as he had been fed by his mother in Spain. I didn't care who raised her. Fermina would be like a sister. That's how it is on our ranch. Animals, people, land, water, plants, trees, bugs, fish, birds—we all belong to each other.

* * *

Mornings in the sheep wagon, pale light from the kerosene lamp made Fermina's dark skin turn yellow. From bed I watched her fill the teakettle, boiling water for Pedro's coffee and hot chocolate for us. A sheep wagon is like a tiny ship. There's a bunk bed across the back with a window, a built-in table, a small wood-stove, and Dutch doors at the front. Water is hauled in a galvanized bucket. I loved the way the tin dipper floated on top of the water like a boat. Sometimes, watching it, Fermina and I talked about hopping a freighter and going around the world, which was funny, since we had never even seen the ocean.

Fermina and I are so different: she's four years younger, dark-haired, dark-eyed, and small for her age, and sometimes speaks a blend of Spanish and English so fast I can hardly understand what she's saying. On the other hand, I'm blond, blue-eyed, and tall and live with my parents in the ranch house, a hundred-year-old log cabin where my father was born. Fermina lives in the sheep wagon with Pedro summers, weekends, and vacations and stays with us in the house on school days so she can ride the bus with me.

"Happy Birthday, Timmy," she said to me, and held out a cupcake with a lighted candle. It was my thirteenth birthday. A weird number for a weird age. I feel like someone stuck between floors in an elevator—not quite grown up, but no longer a child. I know I have to stop doing certain things—like sleeping on the floor with the dogs, trotting out to the corrals pretending that I am a horse. It doesn't matter. The truth is, I don't feel like doing those things anymore; I'm growing into a new body. The same me, but different. Sometimes I wonder if the new me, the-same-but-different me, should have a new name. Should I change it? My mother named me for a cowboy she had ridden with while growing up on a ranch over the mountains, but that Timmy was a man, and I'm a girl.

Outside, sheep began bleating. There was a bang on the side of the wagon, then Pedro's white horse stuck his head through the doorway, wiggling his upper lip, begging for cookies. "Here you go, Whitey," Fermina said, handing him a piece of her cupcake. The candle on mine was still burning, and a little puddle of pink wax formed at the base. I closed my eyes, made a wish, and blew it out. "What did you wish for?" Fermina asked. I shook my head. "If I tell, it won't happen." But secretly, it was this: that nothing would change; that we would all be on this ranch together forever.

The metal roof of the sheep wagon began rattling: a wind had come up. Snow sprayed across the floor as the door opened: Pedro came in. His beard was frosted white. He stoked the stove. He had high cheekbones and a nose and mouth that looked carved. I thought of him as looking saintly—serious and tender and almost gaunt. The first time I saw him he was standing on a ridge in a storm with his arms outspread, singing to the sheep. He poured a cup of coffee and sat on the bench, warming himself. "A storm, she is coming now, pretty big," he said. "I better get these little sheeps nice and fat and full of hay before that happens. You girls help me now, then we will go back to the ranch while we can still see the road."

We dressed quickly and pulled on insulated coveralls over our jeans, flannel shirts, and sweaters. Outside, all was still. I loved the quiet of winter. It was as if the whole world had been laid out flat in front of me and I could see and hear everything. The sun was low. Snow had drifted into round lumps hardened by wind. It shone like a silver and pink skin. Two ravens flew by, their wings creaking, then flapping. They soared, cawing back and forth: *cr-r-uck, cr-r-uck*, then a metallic *tok . . . tok*. Over the next ridge they turned, dropped, rolled, then shot upward: this was the ravens' courtship dance, which happened every February.

We fed the last of the hay to the sheep from the back of the pickup truck. As they trotted behind, bleating, I had a strange feeling: that everything was changing, about to be lost. It was like a knife turning in me. But even as the truck bumped along, there was still a floor under my feet. I only had to keep my balance as we were moving. I started laughing. Then I yelled so loud from happiness that the sheep stopped in their tracks. This made me smile. I leaned down and pushed off flake after flake of hay.

After the sheep had been fed, we drove to the ranch house. The snow squeaked when we walked. The inside of my nose was so cold it hurt to breathe deeply. The sun had vanished, and at the edge of the horizon, snowclouds loomed thick as a mountain range, marching into our valley from a very long way away. I looked at the thermometer: 25 degrees below zero. Half an hour later it had risen to 0. That sudden rise meant snow.

Our ranch lies in a high valley with willow-lined ponds on the edges and sharp-fisted mountains that rise straight up behind the house. To the south and west, a hundred miles away, are more mountains, not a single range, but intersecting islands of them, as if they had been dropped down by a huge hand, splattering here and there. The valleys between are wide, cut up into ribbons by rivers and streams; and at almost every time of year, elk and deer pass through, stopping to graze, drink, swim, or lie down to rest. When the ponds near the house thaw in late spring, wild ducks come, and sand-hill cranes fly in from the south, circling and circling before settling down for the summer on one little bright patch of water to raise their young.

The ranch house is a hundred years old, made of small hand-hewn logs milled straight on the inside. The homesteader had cut the trees in the mountains by himself and carted the logs by wagon to the vertical edge, where he dropped them down a chute of rock and picked them up at the bottom, then carried them here.

There are springs all over our land. The original homesteader dug a shallow well by hand in the 1890s. We still get our water from it today. In Wyoming you have to live where there is good water, because most of the state is a high desert with only eight or ten inches of rain a year.

When my great-grandparents bought the ranch they changed very little. It passed to my grandparents, who lived the same way. Grandad always said that all he had was two pairs of cowboy boots one for dancing and one for working, and that he didn't need anything else. My dad and mom are the same. We don't buy much. In this business, Dad says, you have to be conservative in everything, because it might not rain or snow for seven years or the cattle prices might drop, or sickness might spread through the herd. You have to live like a coyote, he always says. Make your own way with what you have.

My parents aren't at all alike. Mom gets involved in all kinds of political activities, always talking to different groups, trying to find solutions and make peace. Dad teases her and calls her "The Mayor."

Dad likes to stay close to the ranch. He's rarely spent the night anywhere else. Says he'd drive all night just to be there at dawn. He doesn't rest easy if he's away. Winters, Dad repairs tack and makes chaps and saddles and braided reins. Mom cooks on a hundred-year-old wood-burning cookstove. In winter there is always soup or stew and coffee simmering there. Between homework assignments, I spend a lot of time splitting kindling wood for my mother. The pieces have to be just right, especially when she is making a pie or bread. Pedro, who has worked for our family since he was a teenager, taught Fermina and me how to use an axe. He said we had to learn, because we might get snowed in by ourselves one day, and we had to know how to survive.

How to ranch and how to live in the wild have been passed down through the generations of my family and through those who work here as well. Pedro knows many things. How to talk to a dog, a ewe, or a horse and have them understand. He can calm any animal, but he can not calm himself. Sometimes he sleeps out on the ground with the sheep or stays up for many nights if there is a bear or mountain lion around. He knows how to whittle a horse from a piece of pine, how to make tortillas, how to whistle with a piece of grass between his teeth, and once in a while he remembers the dreams which tell him about things to come—bad weather, fires, or someone being born or dying.

That Sunday, when we got back to the ranch, Pedro stood in the yard, looked at the sky, and crossed himself. "*Por favor*, have mercy on us," he said. I asked him why we needed mercy, and he said, "The sheeps were acting strange for a whole week. Maybe a pretty bad thing is coming." But what? I asked. He said nothing, but his eyes glistened.

Mom made a big dinner: meatloaf, mashed potatoes, and a cherry pie, my favorite. Pedro and my father talked about the sheep and horses.

Halfway through the pie we heard it: a banging, like sheet metal falling from the sky. Pedro crossed himself. But that wasn't unusual. He crossed himself before he got on a young horse in the spring and before eating a meal. Dad went to the window. The snowclouds had turned black, and a wind wrenched the night sky into a whirling dervish that would not let up all night.

Pedro stood up abruptly. "I have to get back to my sheeps," he said. He hadn't even finished his meal. He thanked my mother, then hugged Fermina good-bye. We watched him leave from the upstairs window, watched his tail lights vanish in swirling snow.

Fermina and I slept in the same room. The windows shook so violently we pushed our beds together and put on extra down comforters. After a while, the shaking wind seemed more like an embrace than a scolding—it rocked us to sleep.

What was it that woke me? It was dark. Then I heard the silence. As if the world had a thick wad of padding wrapped around it. I looked out the window and couldn't believe my eyes: snow had drifted halfway up the side of the house. Downstairs was white. Wind had driven snow in under the doors and windows that drifted into tiny white pyramids on the floor.

The electricity was off and the pipes had frozen. A stream of water spurted across the kitchen, and the water froze to the floor. I started a fire in the woodstove and stoked the logs in the big one. Then I woke my parents. It had snowed three feet between midnight and dawn and was still snowing. They dressed quickly. "I'm going to go check Pedro, you and Mom and Fermina try to get to the cattle and horses. The wagon is loaded. All you have to do is feed. And don't worry, there won't be any school today. Couldn't get there even if you wanted to," Dad said, and winked.

The snow was so deep that walking was more like wading. In some places snow came up to my waist. I went back to the house, untied my grandad's snowshoes from the living room wall, adjusted the straps, and made my way to the corrals.

I hopped on the back of the flatbed truck. All four tires were chained up, but halfway to the pasture, it bogged down in a snowdrift and wouldn't budge. We got off, looked at how deeply we were stuck, then decided to bring the cows to the hay, rather than the other way around. Even this small task took two hours. Fermina and I tromped snow into a flat trail leading to the lower pasture where the cattle were. I yelled to them, and not knowing what else to do, they came to us.

We cut baling strings and dumped flakes of hay, like loaves of bread, down to the cattle. In some places the hay disappeared in deep snow. We flattened a wide circle with our snowshoes, spreading straw along with alfalfa for the cattle to lie on after eating. There was no running water nearby. They would have to eat snow instead, but they would survive.

The snow came fast in flakes so big they looked like fists. Then, when the temperature dropped in the afternoon, it coarsened into corn snow. The wind picked up. What had been the front pasture, the corrals, and road was wiped away—wiped into a whiteness we could not penetrate. Dad was still gone. We fed the horses again and stood out on the road trying to get a glimpse of headlights, but there were none. Should we go look for him, could we? The road was drifting shut. Mom decided that he'd probably gone to Pedro's camp but just couldn't get back. It wouldn't be safe to go now, she said. "But what if he broke down somewhere?" I asked. There were so many stories of people freezing to death just a few yards from their back doors. The skin on Mom's face flinched, but she said calmly, "We'll just have to hope that didn't happen."

No one talked. We heated up the remains of my birthday dinner, but it was hard to eat. Later, I tried to remember all the Februarys in my life. What they had been like, how bad weather had peeled back into spring. Mostly what I remembered was the silence. It was what I called winter music: a whole orchestra playing with no sound. I noticed in the drifts tiny snow fleas jumping around—a sure sign of spring, since they provide the first food for incoming birds. But there were no birds yet, and I wondered how many had been killed by the blizzard.

Fermina was worried that the bald eagles' eggs, just laid, had been buried in snow. But that night we had bigger worries: had Dad made it to Pedro's, had Pedro made it to his wagon, were they alive? Had the sheep survived? There was no way to know.

At dawn I heard the door opening and feet stamping. "Dad?" I cried out. "It's me," he said. We ran to greet him. Was Pedro all right, and the sheep? "Yes," he said. "Everything is fine. I had to wait out the storm." Mom came in. He looked at her: "And that's a heck of a small bunk Pedro has in that old sheep wagon," he said, laughing. Mom lit the kindling in the cookstove and put on water to boil.

That afternoon I heard Canada geese and saw the first mountain bluebird. Blizzard or not, I knew the bluebird would be okay. Because the sun had come out and there was a hatch of bugs for him to eat, and there were always the snow fleas.

MARCH. *Snow, hot sun, then wind that could carry you away if you didn't hang on. It's the month when the songbirds come back, when calves and lambs are born, all at once, almost always at night or at dawn. It's the sleepless month, when the light stays longer and longer with some days as hot as summer and others as cold as Christmas. Everything wakes up in March. That's why people born in March are so agitated and active, Pedro says. Birds come back—so many I lose count:*

red-winged blackbirds, meadowlarks, bluebirds, redtail hawks, grosbeaks, rosy finches, Cassin's finches, Brewer's blackbirds, and pine siskins. Great horned owls lay their eggs. Stinging nettles green up, and there are butterflies, which Pedro says look like tiny cathedrals. Aspen and cottonwood buds get thick, ready to explode with green leaves. Ermines change their color from white to brown as the snow melts, and snakes entwine when they mate. If it stays warm for a few days, the bears come out of their dens and sniff around, turn over a log to look for grubs, then go back in before the next storm dumps snow. March makes me feel like those bears: nostalgic for winter coziness, but longing for summer sun and skies that stay light half the night.

✳ ✳ ✳

March 6. Mom and Dad took turns checking the heifer pen every two hours all night. The first calf came at dawn. I followed Dad down to the pasture. The young cow was scared. She kept turning her head and looking around as if asking, what's bothering me? Labor didn't last long—a few hours. We had time to go back to the house and eat breakfast before checking her again. What you have to look for, Dad told me, is the feet: calves are born front feet first, like divers, and if the feet come out upside down, it means the calf is turned; or if you only see a tail, the calf is backward. Both situations mean trouble.

The calf's black feet appeared pointing down, then the whole head came out, wet and gooey; and after a few hard pushes, the shoulders passed through. In a few seconds the calf was on the ground. The heifer turned to look: she couldn't believe her eyes. As soon as she saw her calf, the expression on her face changed from one of terror and irritation to one of relief and love. She licked the calf's back. That's to help the respiratory system, Dad told me. The calf shook his head and his ears flopped, making a smacking sound.

In a minute or so, the calf tried to stand. He

was wobbly and fell over the first time, but kept trying. He knew what he wanted. The heifer stood quietly as the calf searched around—first between her front legs, then all around her belly—until finally he found a teat, and there he stayed.

First milk is the most important. It has all the nutrients and hormones to insure that the immune system functions and that the calf will grow and thrive. Without it, he might die. We watched until nose and mouth were wet from the milk. I loved his white stockings and the two little arcs of white above his eyes. Which is why I called him "Eyebrows." I name all the calves.

All through March, in the afternoons before it got dark, we rode through the whole herd looking for the cows who looked "calvy" and brought them to the pasture closest to the house. At night, someone checked the heifer pen every two hours, twenty-four hours a day. Mom did it for a week, then Dad, and sometimes Fermina and I filled in at night after school when my parents got really tired.

March is the month when we have to be on our best behavior, because without much sleep, everyone gets pretty cranky. "Don't you two start getting squirrely," Dad warned, "because your mother is tired." Some days she started crying at the least little thing, but she'd always begin laughing and waving her hand and saying, "Don't mind me."

I loved the nights Fermina and I were on duty even though it was hard to stay awake. Sometimes we took naps and set an alarm clock. The stars looked like a net that had been dropped down: close, dense, and bright. We learned some of the constellations—there was the Big Dipper, of course, and the Pleiades, but our favorite was Orion. His belt flew across the middle of the night sky, and when it went down in the west, we knew it was almost morning. After those long nights we were allowed to skip school and sleep until noon. Then we got up and helped give vitamin shots to newborn calves and do afternoon chores—feed hay and lay out straw for the calves to lie on.

Every few days a meadowlark woke me. Almost nothing in the world made me as happy. Partly because the song was beautiful, and also because I knew, without even looking, that after months of snow and below-zero weather, spring was here. It's easy to see meadowlarks: they are large birds with yellow chests blazed with a black V who like to perch on top of fence posts. When they sing, they throw their heads back as if searching for high C.

What makes me least happy is March mud. As soon as the thaw comes out of the ground, there is no easy way to get from one part of the ranch to the other or to town. Sometimes Dad has to drive us partway down the mountain on the tractor. Our pickups get stuck, and our feet. We look like circus figures with mud balled up on our boots, riding the pastures on horses that are caked in mud.

Each of us has at least three horses, because you can't ride the same horse every day. Mine are called Blue, Chile, and Rockchuck, all quarter horses bred to work cattle. We wear special clothes during calving—insulated coveralls and high, insulated cowboy overshoes that fit over our boots. The mud mixes in with the blood and goo, and when calving is over, we throw all the clothes in a pile and take them to town to the commercial washing machines, then go to the bar for pizza and a soda and a game of pool.

March 15. Everything went so wrong today I didn't know if we would ever recover. It started with a heat wave: temperatures surged to 73 degrees. Two feet of snow melted in one day, and we found calves drowning in standing pools of water. We moved the herd to a hillier pasture so the meltwater would run off faster. But when the wind started up at the end of the day, there was no shelter. We spread straw like crazy. Half of it blew away. We clocked the wind at 85 m.p.h. Then the clouds came in fast, and by dinner, it had begun to snow.

Sudden extremes of weather bring on

pneumonia. Dad and Mom decided we should go out and check the calves. If they were breathing fast—a kind of panting—that meant they were sick. We carried a bag filled with vials of penicillin and plenty of syringes and needles. Giving shots is easy. It's something you do plenty of if you're on a ranch. A cow's hide is thick—they hardly feel the prick. My theory is, if it doesn't hurt them, it doesn't hurt me.

At night the mother cows lie in a circle with their calves in the middle to break the wind and protect the calves from predators, like coyotes, mountain lions, and bears. One of the nights Fermina and I did rounds, we heard coyotes singing and a mountain lion cry out. We slogged through mud. A crust of thin ice had formed over the meltwater. Even Fermina, who weighed only 82 pounds, broke through.

One calf needed a shot. We brought her and her mother into a shed where we had spread fresh straw. We doctored the calf, then went home to our own warm beds. The log walls of the house shifted and whistled as the spring wind blew. Once during the night I woke, got up, pushed my flannel nightgown into my coveralls, and went out to check the calf. He was sleeping peacefully against his mother.

"Timmy! Fermina!" Not the usual wake-up call: I could tell something was wrong. It was just getting light, and a blizzard was raging. Mom and Dad had already been out. They were warming their hands over the cookstove. Mom didn't say anything. Then Dad spoke: "All the calves are dead and a few of the cows. Suffocated. There's four feet of snow. The drifts are ten feet deep."

Everything went silent and swirling at the same time. I couldn't think, I couldn't understand what had happened. Fermina began crossing herself and crying, but I couldn't move. "What do we do now?" I finally asked. Mom looked at me, then away. "I don't know," she said. Then I saw her shoulders move: she was crying. Dad looked calm, but I knew he was badly shaken. He said, "We have to save the rest of the animals now." That began a day I'll never forget: a day on which I worked harder than any other.

Much of the morning was spent making trails through the snow. Dad's bulldozer was at the mechanic's in town, and we sure could have used it. So everything was done by hand and on foot. We stepped into our cross-country skis and tromped snow down, packing it hard so the calves would have some place to stand and eat if and when we ever got to them.

We poked long poles into the drifts to make sure no animals were there and turned the horses out, cutting fence lines with our fencing pliers. Everything looked so different. I felt as if I had moved during the night and this was a new ranch, and I had to learn my way around.

We found a cow giving birth in the middle of the day. The calf dropped down into a deep drift, almost disappearing, and we dove in after it and pulled it out with a rope around its back legs until its mother could lick it dry. Fermina and I carried bales of hay to an area we had flattened out with our skis, one of us on one side and one of us on the other. How many did we carry that day? I don't know, but soon it was getting dark, and the cattle hadn't even eaten.

Mom and Dad were also on skis and they brought the cattle to us. The cows ran when they smelled the hay. Fourteen of them looked like they would calve that night. We spread straw for them to sleep on. That's what low barometric pressure does—it brings on the babies. We hoped they could hold on for another day, but they didn't.

We went home for dinner and drank a gallon of water—so thirsty from all that work, and almost too tired and too dehydrated to eat. We ate without pleasure; we ate because we needed the food.

It was still snowing when the calves began to drop. We skied between cows in the dark with miner's lights on our heads. Every time we found a calf, we rubbed it all over with straw to help dry it off, because sometimes they freeze to the ground if they don't get up quickly. Also,

I found a tiny, migratory bird—a Wilson's phalarope—buried in the snow. When I uncovered it, it looked up at me in surprise and flew away.

The snow kept coming, and we kept tromping it down. I felt as if the world was rising like a loaf of bread, rising, never to stop. Surely we would all drown. At least it was warmer when it was snowing, that's all I could think of.

After two days the storm cleared and the thermometer dropped: from twenty above to twenty below. That night three calves were born, and their wet hides froze to the ground. We got them up and transported them to the house on my old sled, retrieved from the barn. During calving, we always had a calf or two warming up in the kitchen.

Other calves contracted scours—an infection that causes diarrhea. In the spring, during the thaw, our ranch road was sometimes impassable. That's why we couldn't ask the vet to come look at the calves. Anyway, we couldn't afford him. He helped us, free of charge, over the phone, and when we ran out of antibiotics we made our own concoctions, and they worked. This time, the vet and I invented a mixture of beef consommé (because of the gelatin), egg, and Land O' Lakes powdered milk. Mom and I warmed it on the stove, then poured the mixture into Seven-Up bottles and stuck black nipples on.

Some calves were so sick their mouths were cold by the time I got to them. They couldn't stand or suck from a bottle. I'd push the black nipple in, work their mouths with my hand, until one by one, I got food down their throats. One calf was so tiny and dehydrated, I used an eyedropper to get liquid into his mouth. He drank a little but, exhausted from the effort, quietly died in my arms. Why couldn't we do more for them? I hated our crude ways. "It's not fair!" I yelled out to no one in particular and lay back against a cow who was in labor, and covered my face with both hands. When Mother saw me, she stopped what she was doing, came over, and held me. Then we both cried—not just for that calf—but for all the animals who had suffered in these storms. We had lost so many, and we were tired. Later, we came on a mother cow grieving for her dead calf lying stiff in the snow. When we tried to drag the calf away, she bellowed and fought us off. She guarded her baby for three days.

The last week of March another storm descended on us, and we lost more animals. I dreamed about a tree, a weeping willow blowing in the wind. Its branches looked like shoulders heaving. After that, spring came.

THREE

APRiL *is not exactly spring, but that rubbery time between winter and summer. The creeks are frozen, snowstorms fly by, it rains, heats up, cools off, and the wind blows. It's the time when ravens lay their eggs and the great horned owl eggs laid in March have begun to hatch. Ground squirrels come out of their holes, sage grouse do their strutting dance, hawks build huge stick nests on boulders and in cottonwood trees, Canada geese and sandhill cranes circle*

every pond, looking for a place to lay eggs. Up in the high country, grizzly bears peek out of their dens to see what they can see. The south slopes of every mountain melt off and erupt in white phlox, blue forget-me-nots, and wild carrot, and along the creeks, bulrushes begin to grow. Late in the month there are more hawks and kestrels. Elk begin migrating to higher altitudes, deer give birth, and on the rivers, mergansers sit on their eggs.

April is branding time, when all the neighbors get together, rope, vaccinate, brand, and castrate calves, then eat a big picnic meal. The short, cold-weather grasses come on up, and spring roundup begins—not really a roundup but a "turning out," because it means we take the cows and calves out onto spring range.

✳ ✳ ✳

April 4. A herd of fifty elk moved through the ranch this morning. They were big and grayish-brown and held their heads high like royalty. "They look awfully snooty, don't they," Mother said, laughing. The least little sound spooked them, so we tiptoed around the ranch, keeping silent while we did chores so as to be able to watch them for a long time.

Later, Dad and I rode young horses—a two-year-old colt and a three-year-old filly. Young horses can be dangerous if you haven't worked them right. A horse will buck or run away if they get scared—not because they're mean but out of self-defense. We ride them in the round corral first, what Dad calls working with their minds—and bodies, too—getting some flexibility, a soft feel with the reins, and developing a feeling of trust and confidence between us.

When I first got on, the colt began to buck, but instead of pulling up on the reins like the old-timers do, I let the reins loose, then gave him a job to do. He jumped a few jumps, and quickly forgot about being scared. Dad smiled and nodded at me, then we tipped our horses into a trot and kept going for quite a few miles.

Later in the day we visited a hermit. He lives on a hill in a barnlike house with no electricity, running water, or phone, and he smells bad because he never bathes. His paintings and sculptures of horses are wonderful, though, and I always like seeing him. That day as we talked he did a drawing for me, of my horse Rockchuck and the mountain behind us, with its cornices sending snowflags into the sky.

He has no car, and when he rides his donkey he refuses to use a saddle or bridle. Says it is cruel to the animal. He rode halfway home with us bareback, guiding the burro with a loose string around its nose. I invited him to come home with us for dinner. He said, "Ohhhh noooo . . . this has been enough excitement for one day." Another year would go by before we visited him again. Anything more would have been an invasion of his privacy, Mom said.

April is branding time. The ranchers in the valley schedule brandings together and on the weekends, we go from ranch to ranch, herd to herd, neighbors helping each other. The night before our branding, Pedro, Dad, and I rode out and brought all the cows and calves into a holding pasture with plenty of water and feed. Mom and Fermina stayed home and made enchiladas, pies, and salads. In the morning, I rode my cutting horse, Chile, and helped separate the calves from their mothers. The calves were moved into the branding pen. Pedro had already started the branding fire. The irons lay in the flames getting hot. Neighbors arrived. We put out urns of coffee and ice chests full of pop and beer, and backed a pickup to the fence with all the vet supplies.

Dad was in charge: he decided who was going to rope and for how long: four men at a time went into the pen with eight of us kids on the ground to hold the calves. Soon the great O's of lariat loops soared through the air. Calves were heeled and dragged by their hind legs to the branding fire. Syringes were filled with vaccines and vitamins, shots were given, bulls were castrated, then the heel loop was loosened, and the calves were sent on their way.

During the morning everyone was given a chance to rope, and Dad was good at pairing young and old, experienced and inexperienced. He never made a show of it, but he always had his eye on everyone.

Usually we were finished by midafternoon. It was different at our branding this year. So few calves had survived the storms, branding only took a few hours. No one said anything. Many ranchers had suffered losses, but none as great as ours—our ranch was higher up in the mountains, and we'd had deeper snow. Regardless of numbers, the work went quickly—no more than two minutes per animal. And afterward, we enjoyed a feast of roast beef, enchiladas, beans, rice, tortillas, salad, and pie—and lots of storytelling.

Then there was a baseball game. We used elk legs left over from hunting season for bases. We played by cowboy rules: When I hit a home run, the guys ran over, picked me up, and carried me around to home base, then touched me with the baseball and put me out. We never took stuff like winning very seriously, because we knew the difference between work and play and had learned from the older cowboys how to laugh at ourselves.

Later we danced to The Dixie Chicks and George Strait. I noticed that the guys treated me differently. I closed my eyes as we swayed to the music and remembered the article I'd read about three mountain climbers from Wyoming who were in the news after being caught in an avalanche. They had to swim down the mountain through cascading snow. One of them died. Like the calves this spring, he had suffocated. When the reporter asked the survivors how they were feeling, they said the mountain was a river; it was always moving; it was the same mountain they'd climbed but it had changed; that even standing still at the bottom of the peak, they did not know where they were.

That evening a herd of fifty elk bedded down in our upper pasture. My friends and I sneaked up on them, crawling on our bellies, and lay there watching the animals.

Spring roundup. We begin the slow progression of moving cattle from lower pastures to ones that are higher. It's like climbing a ladder. We were up at 3:30, ate breakfast, made sandwiches, wrangled horses, saddled up, and were trotting down to the holding pens by 4:25. In the dark, we began moving cows and calves to spring range, the foothills of the big mountains where they'd graze in the summer. Something was different this year. As we pushed the cattle through the gate, the banker was there counting animals. At dinner I asked Dad why. I guess I hadn't been thinking very clearly, because it wasn't until then that I understood the financial effect of the blizzards. It was simple: if we had no calves to sell, we had no income, and no money to pay the bank the annual operating costs we borrowed from them every year.

But it wasn't our fault, I told my dad. Can't they give us an extra year or two? He said that even though it wasn't our fault, the banks can't run a business that way. "Either you have the money or you don't, that's all they care about."

I objected. "But I go to school with that banker's kid—we're all friends," I said. Dad smiled and said, "We're going to be all right, we just have to tighten our belts a little."

I didn't know how our belts could get much tighter: we grew our own food, hunted in the fall, didn't take holidays, drove old pickups that we fixed ourselves, and spent almost nothing on clothes. There weren't any restaurants or movies to go to—just the bar, and we only went there once in a while.

Dad sold some cows this spring—not just the old ones, but some of the good young ones with calves on their sides. He didn't say anything about it, and he didn't have to. I knew what was going on. But the more cows he sold to make bank payments, the fewer calves we would have to sell next year.

It looked bad to me. I dreamed about a terrible storm: a big downward spiral, like a tornado, dark and turbulent, filled with cattle, dogs, horses, and me. What is odd is that spring fills me with such happiness. The songbirds were coming back and swallows built their mud nests in the corner of the eaves. Two snakes did a mating dance in front of the kitchen window, twisted together in a knot with only their heads free. Ermines shed their white coats and turned brown. Deer browsed on mountain mahogany. But we are losing the ranch, and I don't see how these two things could go on at the same time, how a season when everything is filling up again fits with a ranch that is dwindling.

High winds. A storm came fast, then bolted away. In the sun, I rode down the mountain to an abandoned homestead. I smelled something wonderful. What was it? Where did it come from? Then I saw the row of irises that had sprouted on the ditchbank. I got off Blue and picked some—one purple, one yellow, and another almost black. Blue liked the way they smelled. I don't know if he can see the colors. I held them under my nose all the way home.

That night I heard Mom and Dad talking late into the night at the kitchen table. It must have been about money, because the adding machine was clicking away. I climbed halfway down the stairs to listen. I think they knew I was there, but they didn't say anything. They weren't fighting, just doing computations: the sale price for pregnant cows, dry cows, steer calves, heifer calves, bulls, as well as sheep, horses, and personal items in the house. Then I heard Dad say there wasn't enough money to save the ranch. Mom said, "No, that can't be right. I'm going to start all over again." And the adding machine began whirring again.

That's when I went back to my room. I sat cross-legged on my bed, eating long ropes of licorice, and thought about what would happen if we had to move away. It didn't seem possible. Where would we go? What would we do? We didn't know how to do anything but ranch. Then, when I thought about the animals—the dogs, horses, cows—I couldn't sit there any longer. A watery wall came down behind my eyes and leaked—I wasn't crying, but my body was.

I ran downstairs, called the dogs, and led them past my parents up to my room and into bed with me. I would stay there with them and not budge, ever. The bank would have to carry us all away.

FOUR

MAY *is the month of apple trees flowering, of meltwater coming down, of Indian paintbrush blooming, of Canada geese and ravens hatching, and blue herons incubating eggs. Larkspur, bluebells, forget-me-nots, and shooting stars bloom. Up in the mountains the elks' antlers are in velvet, coyote pups are growing and playing outside of their dens, all the streams and rivers are running hard, the water, brown as chocolate milk shakes, too turbulent for fishing. It is the month when we work the hardest, irrigating, putting in*

a garden, fixing fences, and riding colts. As snow melts, we continue moving cows and calves, ewes and lambs farther away from the ranch, and higher in the mountains.

* * *

May 1. Today I talked only when spoken to. When I went outside, I could smell the thaw, smell life again. I usually feel so alive at this time of year—but not now, because all was clouded over with the threat of having to leave. It was as if winter had not gone away. How do you leave everything you know and love? I asked Mom. She said, "Don't worry, something will work out," but I wasn't so sure. I stayed out with the animals when I was at home— worked with the young horses, getting them to trust me, did chores: feeding calves, horses, dogs, barn cats, wild birds. The dogs never left my side.

School would be out in the middle of May. They let ranch kids go early so we can help move cattle. School is torture because every minute I am there means I am not on the ranch, and the clock is ticking.

Some days I feel so alone. There is nobody to talk to. Fermina is only nine and doesn't understand about losing the ranch, how the bank could take everything away, just like that—and Mom and Dad are trying to protect me. They don't really tell me what is going on. Instead, I talk to the horses and dogs. They wouldn't leave me or I them. We'd made a pact: when the bankers came, we'd pack up some things and take off over the mountains and keep going.

On Mother's Day the meltwater came down from the high mountains, filling the irrigation ditches with muddy water. Mom and I had been making orange tarp dams—five-foot pieces of reinforced plastic with a hem on one end through which we thread a pole. The dams are laid across the ditch. The pole holds the top end in place, while the loose end is shoveled into the mud at the bottom. When the water comes, it hits the dam and squirts out to one side through a notch and down onto the field. The next day we plug the sod back into the notch and move the dam downstream. In this way, we follow the ditch all the way down to the bottom of the field, spreading water as we go. By the time we get to the end of the ditch, it is time to start all over again. In the spring we put out about thirty dams and these are moved twice a day, every day, until midsummer.

I irrigated two alfalfa fields, and Mom or Dad did the rest. I like it best in the early morning when the birds are singing. Sometimes a rattlesnake comes out of its den and slides along the ditch for a drink of water. We never kill them unless they are right beside the house. After setting a dam, I like to watch the water fan out across the field, sparkling in the sun like diamonds. We may not have any money, but at least we have water.

May 14. School is out. Hurray! Fermina went to stay with Pedro out on the range, and the next day Mom and I started putting the vegetable garden in. It is a quarter of an acre, and during the summer, we freeze enough vegetables to last the winter. I asked my mother why we were bothering. She looked hard at me and said, "We have to take things day by day and not assume too much one way or the other." Sounded like a cover-up to me. But I had no choice. I helped her anyway.

The cold-weather plants went in first: peas, lettuce, swiss chard, spinach, bok choy; then, approaching the full moon, cucumbers, squash, and ten varieties of beans. During the waning moon, we planted root vegetables: carrots, red and yellow beets, radishes, and turnips. Corn we couldn't grow, so we traded green beans for it with neighbors in the valley below.

The days are getting long, but sometimes I wish they were shorter. That way, I could go to bed sooner and sleep instead of working away as if we were going to be here forever. When I asked Dad about the future, he said, "My crystal ball is broke." Then, "And anyway, what if we do stay but haven't done any of the spring work? How would we manage? There'd be fences broken down, and cattle scattered, and no vegetables in the garden, and water just going by, no hay crop. We'd be in a hell of a mess. Anyway, even if we do get foreclosed on, we want to leave the place in good shape. Maybe no one else cares, but we sure as hell do. The land and the animals know, and we can't turn against them even when our luck is down."

As usual, Dad was right, and from then on I began to feel a little better.

May 17. Flash flood. The steep road up to the ranch turned into a red river. Creeks rose fast. They were red walls swallowing everything. Once a shallow ocean covered Wyoming, and today, it seems to be up in the sky, pouring back down.

Later. A cloud captured us. There was nothing visible: no mountains, no fence lines, no pond, no animals, no outbuildings. The electricity went out, too. We didn't care—we cooked on the wood cookstove and lit kerosene lamps all over the house that evening. Dad said he preferred it that way and threatened to have the electricity turned off anyway. Mom laughed and said, "Fine with me, let's go solar." What about in the winter during snowstorms? I asked. Or now, when we sometimes have weeks of rain? How would I power my computer?

Drought and flood: the two extremes are married, my mother said. After the rain, there was instant green as if shaken from a bottle, new grass covering the hills as far as I could see. In the morning there were so many birds, they darkened the sky.

On a misty, silent May 18, a foal was born. I went down to the sheds the night before just before going to bed and saw the mare was in labor. Stayed up all night with her. Slept in a pile of straw, then went and got Dad when the foal started coming. So much can go wrong with mares having foals, but we lucked out this time. The little hooves showed, then the wet head, the long ears plastered back. It was a blue roan stud-colt with coal-dark eyes and eyelashes half an inch long. Everything was so perfectly formed, the bones in his face, his ears, legs, and tail, I could have looked at him for the rest of my life. This is happiness.

May 25. A big, soggy, long-winded rain closed in. Clouds so low we couldn't see the mountains. Land shaved flat, as if we lived on the great plains. It rained for five days. Dad and Mom became absolutely quiet about losing the ranch. I guess they didn't want to upset me, or maybe there was just nothing else to say. Our problem was like a big tight cloud stretched above our heads and my thinking kept bumping up against it. I could see it was on their minds—the hard way their jaws were set, like the jaw of a horse that's about to run away. I spent quite a bit of time between chores in the barn with the mare and foal. I named him "Black 'n' Blue." He reminded me that good things can still happen in the midst of the bad.

For the next week we would get up at 3:30 A.M.
Dad "jingled" the horses (went to get them out
of the lower pastures) while Mom and I made
sandwiches, which we usually ate by 10:30 A.M.
We were on horseback by 4:15 in the morning.
It was still dark when we left at a hard trot. It
took two hours just to get to the cattle. As light
filled the sky everything was in silhouette—I
liked that—horses' heads, cottonwood trees bent
over a spring, eagles flying up, nighthawks
zooming down. No one talked. We were too
sleepy and rattled by hours of trotting. An odd-
shaped, egg-shaped orange moon set as the sun
rose. I rode in a trance: once I nodded off and
dreamed we would still be here next year.

It usually took ten to fourteen days to move
all the cattle and sheep into the higher pastures
of spring range, but this year we would do it in
just a few. We looked silly with our tiny bunch
of cows and calves and sheep. "Like home-
steaders," Dad said, and he didn't mean it kindly.

Spring range is the high desert foothill

country that turns into alpine mountains. I love it almost more than the high country—at least in the spring. The grass was stirrup-high, Indian paintbrush bloomed everywhere, tiny creeks wound around outcrops of rock—creeks that, in another month, would be dry. Here and there, shallow ponds held pairs of mallards. Three antelope joined the herd for a few miles, then darted off running as only antelope can run. We wound through narrow, red-rocked canyons, then took a twisting trail up onto mesas that jutted into the sky. Ahead were snowcapped mountains. These mesas were true mansions—the only ones I would ever live in. I thought that, forgetting that we might lose it all.

FIVE

JuNE *is true spring in the northern Rockies—not April or May the way it is in other places. At high altitudes we have to wait longer for warm sun and spring wildflowers, and we lose it sooner. But the beauty, when it comes, is that much richer. The light is pale and clear and the sun is a hot hand that touches you, healing all of winter's wounds.*

June means high water: by the time the spring runoff overfills the creeks, chokecherry trees blossom, birds mate and nest, and the young ones begin fledging. Barn swallows build their mud houses, a first clutch of mallard ducklings hatches out; butterflies flit around, king snakes and rattlesnakes slither into holes and out onto sunny rocks, always trying to stay warm. Gooseberry bushes put out blossoms shaped like bells which ring the bears in, deer and elk calves are born, and higher up, moose calves wobble through willows. The native grasses on which the cattle, horses, and elk thrive, come in stages like acts in a play. The grasses don't live long but are potent, palatable, and full of protein, each species delicate and beautiful and unique, as if the hardship of cold winters pushed them toward a higher excellence. That's what this spring beauty is all about: it's a richness your mind can grow fat on without having to eat.

✻ ✻ ✻

All day Dad and I moved cattle. Just after dawn, as we rode past a steep, rocky slope, four baby coyotes emerged from their den. They stretched and yawned, but when they saw me on my horse, they sat down, their long ears pointed sharply. Too young to be afraid, too shy to inspect me. We just stared at each other, then I moved on.

Cowboying is fast and exciting, and moving sheep is slow, like music. The next day I rode with Pedro and Fermina. We took the ewes and lambs to a higher pasture. At midday, when it was hot, they stood in a knot with their heads together and wouldn't move. So from eleven in the morning until three in the afternoon, we lay on the ground under a cottonwood tree by a creek and told stories.

Pedro told us about cowboying in Mexico when he was a young man. How they'd had a burro that carried the flour and water, and at night, they'd make tortillas and wrap a piece of jerky in them, and that was their meal.

As he talked, the sheep dozed, then slowly began to fan out over the range and graze. We saddled up again and gently moved them into the upper country near good water and fresh grass. Pedro grew silent and looked sad. "Are we going to lose it all?" I asked. He shrugged, "Maybe. I don't know. It's pretty bad, but I have been asking for it not to be so," he said, crossing himself and looking upward. That evening, in the sheep wagon, I saw the tiny cross he'd made from braided willow branches. It rested against the kerosene lamp. He made dinner: fried mutton burger, onions, tomatoes, and homemade tortillas. Fermina and I sat on the bunk across the back of the wagon and ate. I guess we were thinking the same thoughts about losing the ranch and being separated, because we both started crying. I wanted to live with her and Pedro always. We hugged each other until we laughed and Pedro opened his long arms and hugged us both.

That night, sleeping out under the stars in our white canvas bedrolls, I felt weightless and empty, like tin foil blowing around in the wind, creasing and tearing in flight. When I woke in the morning, there was no breeze. The sun had come on hard. I wondered where we would go

if we lost the ranch, but couldn't visualize anything. Just a blank, a windstorm, a ground blizzard. I looked around: Fermina and Pedro
weren't in their beds. I felt like the last person
on earth.

Mid-June. Bugs aren't too bad yet. Hot sun.
Grass going to seed. Wild roses in bloom.
Swallows nesting in the eaves. I listened to
swallow talk: *kvik-kvik, vit-vitk, keet—*. They
sounded so human and liked to live close to us.
If this were my ranch, I'd let them build their
nests inside the house. If we lived where it was
warm, I wouldn't have any walls at all.

One night at dinner, when Mom and Dad
were talking about finances, I asked what the
banker had said lately. Dad looked at me. "Well,
banks are fine, but they're kind of narrow-
minded, and that means they aren't very sym-
pathetic." How can you change no cattle into
money? I didn't ask again.

On the range, I watched the momentary
islands a cloud's shadow made. How quickly

they were erased, as if from a blackboard. Sky turned black and clouds rolled over steep hills. So cold we lit the woodstove. More rain with a few snowflakes mixed in. Summer tried to come but failed.

Summer solstice. The longest day of the year. What Pedro calls, "*El día largo.*" The long day. Dad says, "The trouble is, it means winter is on the way again." Someone must have heard him and turned on the snow machine, because it snowed during the night and stuck in the rim-rocks above the ranch. There was light in the sky until 10:30 P.M.

Another night. Went to sleep to the sound of rain and woke up to thunder and lightning and a raging wind that didn't howl, but shook and knocked at things, as if trying to break the last bits of winter away. There were wildflowers in bloom—sego lilies, Indian paintbrush, lupine, wild rose. And two mallard ducks on the pond with a total of eleven babies.

Every day we irrigated hayfields. That

meant setting dams early in the morning, then changing them again in the evening. We each had our own fields to tend to. Dad had to cut the shovel handles down for Fermina and me so we wouldn't break our jaws if the ends hit us.

Before we knew it, it was time to cut hay. Everyone helped. Dad drove the mower, Mom drove the baler, and some kids from the valley helped Fermina and me stack the bales. Even Brandon, the banker's son helped. He had the biggest smile of anyone I knew—how was it possible that his father would take everything away?

Early mornings, late nights—that's what June meant, since it has the longest day of the year. We barbecued almost every night, because it felt so good to be outside after a long winter. Up in the high country above the ranch, elk and deer grazed in small pocket meadows and slept in the shade of pine and aspen trees during the heat of the day; and up top, the mountains made of snow let loose and drained away.

SIX

JULY is the center of the year, the fat middle of summer, the equator where it gets so hot you can fry an egg on the hood of the pickup—I know because Dad did it one day, then tried to get us to eat it. July is when everything is blooming, hatching, going to seed. Baby bald eagles are learning to fly, pine pollen wafts in yellow clouds, cottonwood fuzz clouds the streams, and in the high country, whole meadows of wild iris dry up and knock together like castanets, while other flowers weave into a thick *carpet. Young birds are leaving their nests—wrens, robins, swallows, sparrows, kestrels, warblers, and red-winged blackbirds. Ducklings are born on the pond and soon peek out of the reeds to test their skills at swimming behind their mother. Young ravens have gotten their black, shiny feathers, rattlesnakes are buzzing, and the air is full of bugs: mayflies and mosquitoes, deer- and horseflies, grasshoppers, and butterflies so perfect in design, they look like stained-glass windows. Even at night the world is busy, with night-blooming flowers and nocturnal animals searching for food. July is like the round midsection of an owl.*

* * *

All week we moved cows to the high country, through lodgepole pine forests, up and around granite outcrops where marmots played hide-and-seek with the dogs. The temperature shifted from hot and sultry to cold and crisp, and every afternoon thunderstorms threatened us with snow. We stayed at cow camp. This made it easier to move cattle, fix fences, and sort out the strays on the mountain. It isn't much—a tiny two-room cabin on the top of the mountain where we cook on a woodstove and bathe in a galvanized tub and sleep in beds on a screen porch. No phones, clocks, radios, or TVs. At night we play cards or tell stories. The mosquitoes were bad, but the cool air refreshed us, and our time together on the mountain was always special.

On the Fourth of July, all work stopped and play began. Friends—neighboring ranchers, hired hands, the local doctor, Pedro and Fermina, the banker and his son, Brandon—all came to the cabin to celebrate. There were kids, dogs, horses, even a mule, and buckets full of ice, beer, iced tea, lemonade, and pop, and lots of food—salads, grilled hamburgers and corn, pies and cakes.

During the afternoon we had a horse race. Dad made me ride one of Pedro's sheepherder horses, and he rode a mule. We came in about even, laughing all the way. Later, we played cow-boy polo: mallets, western saddles, and a beach ball so it wouldn't get lost in the sagebrush.

As evening came on, the old-timers—includ-ing Pedro and Dad—told stories. We'd heard them before, but I liked hearing them again. That was the night we kids came up with a solution to my parents' money problem. We waited until the old folks had gone to bed, then we sneaked out to the tack shed and sat in a circle with a kerosene lamp. I explained that Mom and Dad weren't making any headway and that soon our ranch would be foreclosed on. Either that, or we had to sell the ranch now, and no one wanted to do that. So we asked ourselves what the solution might be—outside of banks and borrowing money. Brandon, the banker's son, was there. He didn't care much for town life and wanted to be a rancher. He agreed that we had to get creative. Since there was no way to get money, maybe we could get more cattle. But how? "By computer," Brandon said. "E-mail." After half an hour, we came up with this idea:

We'd send an E-mail to every feed store and western store in the Rocky Mountain west describing the blizzards and our losses and ask if any rancher who was able to would donate a cow and calf, or a yearling, in return for a tax deduction. "How do we get that?" I asked. Brandon said he wasn't sure, but he'd find out from his father. I wasn't clear how all this would work, but it was worth trying. Nothing to lose. And if it worked, our family ranch might make it to the next year.

The trick was this: none of the adults must know what we were doing. Ranchers are proud—too proud, sometimes. Dad would think that asking for free animals from strangers was begging. It was, in a way, but sometimes when you need help, you just have to ask for it, no? Brandon said, "Let's just think of it as neighbors helping each other, even if the neighbors are two states away."

Mid-July. Fermina, Mom, Dad, and I stacked hay for eight hours. During lunch, I watched a single leaf fall from a cottonwood tree, catching and releasing light like a cinder. That's how hot it was—everything was ember or ash. I took a nap under the cottonwood trees until raindrops blasted the hay dust on my arms and face. Jumped up, ran home. Ten ravens flew up out of the trees as though shot from cannons, then dropped, catching themselves midway, only to climb again to the place where the storm had ignited. Later, there was lightning in the part of the sky where they had played.

Fermina and I rode our colts in the afternoon, then Brandon came over under the pretext of working on a 4-H project with me, and we worked on the E-mail asking for donations of livestock.

Writing the message was easy enough, but getting the addresses took longer. By the end of the week it was ready to go. Just before we clicked on SEND, I hesitated: were we doing the right thing? Would my parents hate me? I took a deep breath, then sent it off over the telephone lines to ranchers in Wyoming,

Montana, Idaho, Nevada, and North and South Dakota.

Late July. The heat came on suddenly. Even the mountain was hot. All I could do was sweat. Bugs rained down from the sky—mosquitoes, deerflies, and horseflies that attacked the pickup truck as we drove. Summer was a single bead, a tiny sun dropping down the face of the globe; the inside of the earth was hot mush; the wildflowers were lights going on and off. Starting low in the valley, the bloom crawled up and up, and by the time the flowers at 10,000 feet carpeted the meadows waving yellow, red, blue, and violet blossoms, the ones in the valley and on spring range had already gone out. These were the names of some of them: lupine, harebell, bluebell, yarrow, aster, buttercup, sweet vetch, feverfew, elephanthead, sticky geranium, red monekyflower, Indian paintbrush, cinquefoil, elk thistle, butter-and-eggs, water parsnip, sego lily, blue penstemon.

AUGUST *is the end of something that seems as if it just began. Apple and chokecherry trees have fruit, rose hips are past prime, the edges of streams begin to freeze at night—a necklace of ice. Rabbit brush is bright yellow, fireweed is red, western coneflowers look like monks with shaved heads. Showy asters bloom, especially near the outhouse. Yellow leaves invade every tree, trying to convince summer to end. Fruit, heat, dust—what is it?*

Where does it go when lightning's skywriting stops and the faint blaze in the sky, far away, is summer's heater slowing down?

* * *

My heart is racing. Cicadas clatter, grasshoppers bounce from one side of the field to the other. Light splashes across water, blotching it, then it blazes. In the garden, vegetables jump: beans dangle, squash protrudes, lettuce waves its thin arms.

Brandon called. Had he gotten any E-mails? No. Had I? No. He asked me to go to the County Fair. I said okay. My parents swallowed hard when I told them, because their friendship with Brandon's father had become strained. "What does that have to do with Brandon?" I asked. They smiled. I was right. They said, "Go ahead and have fun." He came to help with chores and off we went.

On the way to the fair we talked about everyone: cowboys, herders, hermits, mechanics, barkeeps, postmasters, railroad people, hardware store clerks—all the people who made up our community. Brandon told me that his dad took groceries out to one of their old herders who wasn't right in his head and couldn't work anymore. The man wouldn't even open the door—you had to leave the box of supplies on the ground and later, when it was safe, he'd come out and get them. But one week, Brandon's father saw that the groceries hadn't been retrieved. He opened the door. The herder was dead. Old age, that's all. The wagon was dark and dank. At the mortuary, they had to peel his long underwear off. He was buried in a plot reserved in the ranch graveyard and given a proper cowboy's funeral, including a rendition of "Home on the Range."

Near the fairgrounds we passed Bob, an old sheepherder who was either too drunk or too bunged-up to herd anymore. He was sitting in front of his house in a plastic chair with his boots and cowboy hat on, dousing himself with water from the lawn sprinkler. "That's a sheepherder's swimming pool," Brandon said.

We walked through the exhibits. I loved the fair. We looked at the animals—chickens, rabbits, steers, lambs, pigs. Usually I had a lamb or steer to show, but we had lost all our 4-H prospects in the blizzard, and so had some of the other kids. This year I was an onlooker. I tried not to feel sad, because this was always a happy day.

We ate hamburgers and homemade pie and looked at the artwork. Later, I won a turkey in a raffle. In the evening we went to the rodeo. We sat above the bucking horse chutes and watched them set their saddles, pull up on the flank strap, and mark the broncs out with their spurs touching the horse's shoulder—otherwise they'd get points marked off. Brandon was a team roper like a lot of kids who lived in town, because they didn't have evening chores and could use the rodeo grounds to practice. He roped in one go-around but missed. He came back to the stands and said, "There must have been a hole in my rope—the steer ran right through it," and laughed.

After, there was a street dance. Mom and Dad and Fermina came and everyone danced with everyone—kids and adults.

The next day. I checked my E-mail. Just a few crackpot messages, that's all. I prayed that Mom and Dad wouldn't find out about our idea. Dad would probably disown me, but that's the risk I had to take. Brandon and the others said they'd come to my defense. Even if it didn't work, even if there was not a single response, then at least I would know I had done something, that I'd tried.

Crow Fair. The annual powwow: a week of dancing, singing, and drumming, plus horse racing on the Crow Indian Reservation northeast of our ranch and over the border in Montana. I went with Fermina and another family. Camped out on the hill. Below was a whole valley filled with white tipis. Though it was the Crow Reservation, many tribes were represented there—Shoshone, Bannock, Arapaho, Kiowa, Navajo, Lakota, Cheyenne, Blackfoot, and more.

They followed the summer powwow circuit—whole families went from place to place dancing all night, sleeping half the day, riding horses in the afternoon. Why couldn't we live like that? I asked Fermina. It gave us a feeling for what their summer encampments all over the northern Rocky Mountain states must have been like during and after the Lewis and Clark days. Of course we were born too late for that. But still . . .

We visited our Arapaho and Shoshone friends whom we knew from basketball tournaments between our schools. Under an arbor made of cottonwood and pine branches, we ate fry bread, roast mutton, cake, and iced tea. Gary, a Crow dancer, worked on his costume: so many beads, it had taken him all winter to make it, he said.

The dancing started at dark with an Indian giveaway: gifts from one family were given to another, things like Pendleton blankets, food, and beadwork. An old Arapaho man told me that once people gave everything away until they had nothing left—no blankets or no horses or food. "That was the best way," he said. "But now, it's different. They give less, and so they get almost nothing back. That is why things are bad now."

Dark. The drummers sat around huge drums and started playing. When I stood close, I could feel the vibrations all the way through my body. They sang in falsettos. The dancers came out, long hair in braids, bright dresses, skirts, moccasins, headdresses—spangled feathers as bright as fireworks. Fermina said that the drumming tapped her heart. I didn't know why, but sometime during the night, all the noise and thrumming made me cry. Drummers from the Navajo Nation played and sang, then the Arapaho, and the Sho-Ban, on and on around the whole dance ground as if around the world. That night, all sound was a form of drumming, all thinking and feeling was spelled out in fancy footwork, and everyone understood.

Late in the night a Crow friend's daughters

asked us to dance with them. We wore our moccasins—Christmas presents from Mother, who always encouraged our friendships with kids from the rez. In turn, they taught us their dances. We stood in a line with other kids our age. We were the only Anglos. Some of the guys wore Wranglers and cowboy boots, others were in fancy dance dress. It didn't matter. The drumming began, and our feet moved, slowly at first. I was a little self-conscious. Then I didn't know what happened; suddenly we were dancing.

Just before dawn, we went to bed. The whole village of tipis had gone quiet. No drumming now. Just the whir of nighthawks and the occasional coyote howling. Lying in my bedroll, I thought about our ranch. Maybe it was being taken from us because we hadn't given enough away. And already, we were begging for something back. I resolved to ask the old man what to do.

Morning. Couldn't find the old man. Went to

his son's camp—he wasn't there. I asked around. No one knew where he was. Fermina and I went to one of the food stands and bought hot dogs wrapped in fry bread. We decided to celebrate Fermina's birthday during Crow Fair every year, so I bought her a present—a pair of dangling turquoise earrings—and a pair for myself, too. We resolved to get our ears pierced. There was another stand down the row that would do it, we were told. We sat on chairs. A Navajo woman held something that looked like a leather punch to my ear. *Boom.* One hole was made. Then the other. It didn't hurt. "Come back in the morning and we'll put your new earrings in," she said.

Another night of dancing. I walked around the circle behind the drums. Fermina was right: they tapped inside me until my chest had ears and the ears started to listen. "All this is ancient music," one old woman told me. The players wore ballcaps and dark glasses, and drank Cokes, but when they sang, it was something else again. High, falsetto voices . . . to make music like that, I wondered, where did it come from?

The new moon set early. Again, I looked for the old man but couldn't find him. Up on the hill, the cottonwood leaves had began to turn. We were flying toward winter and the drumming was pushing us faster and faster. In the dark, in our tent, Fermina and I ate the birthday cake Mom had made for her. "It tastes like the moon," she said, licking white frosting from her fingers. Then we slept, side by side, her dark hair overlapping my blond. I dreamed that all the hour hands on all the clocks in the world spun around and around. When they stopped, there was no ranch, no home. Nothing.

After another all-nighter, it was time to pack up and leave. I walked one last time around the camp. We said good-bye to our friends against whom we would soon be playing basketball. As I passed a clump of cottonwood trees by a little stream, I saw him: the old man. He was sitting in a folding chair drinking a soda.

"You found me," he said. "That's good," and laughed his toothless laugh.

"How did you know I was looking for you?" I asked.

He wrinkled his eyes and smiled but said nothing. Then I didn't know what to say. Just blurt out my question? But what was it? The long silence didn't bother him. He watched a flicker fly from tree to tree, knocking a hole in a dead trunk.

"He's making a house out of nothing," the old man said, looking up at the bird. "He doesn't care which tree it's in. They're all good trees. Maybe that's what you'll have to do."

I stared at him and tried to digest what he had said. Was it about me, or was he just talking?

"But what about the giveaway. How do I do that?"

He squinted hard and burned a look into me, then laughed. "You are too serious."

I must have acted exasperated, because he motioned with his stubby, swollen, wrinkled hand for me to step nearer. Then he said in a gravelly voice: "If you give everything, you get a lot back, and when you are getting things, that's giving, too."

August 10. Back at the ranch we had to jump into work again, and it was only at night that I could think about my "cattle call." So far there were only a few feeble E-mails and no real offers. I tried to think of giving rather than receiving, but nothing jelled. I felt lost—as if the ground had slid out from under me, as if I was treading water.

August 16. Puppies are born. We'd almost forgotten that one of the dogs was pregnant. There were six of them, two black, two brown, and two blond. I'd already picked out the one I wanted, but on the other hand, I preferred keeping them all. There can't be too many of anything when it comes to animals.

I spent a lot of time playing with the dogs when I should have been helping in the garden.

I watched them suckle, explore, fight, and play. The next week their eyes opened. I built a large enclosure in the yard out of straw bales so they couldn't wander away. One year we lost some pups to skunks and rattlesnakes, and I didn't want that to happen again.

At night I brought the whole litter in. They slept in a huge cardboard carton from the grocery store. I could hear them mewling and sucking during the night, which pleased me. But what would we do with six puppies and no place to live? I couldn't think about it. Instead I wondered how receiving could be transformed into giving and if we'd ever get any cows.

August 26. Weather change. Yellow in the cottonwood trees and a lowering sky—not the wild, fast, cursive scrawl of midsummer thunderstorms. These brought slower rains, and the afternoons grew cold. I couldn't believe that soon we'd be back in school. And still no offers to replenish our herd. I had failed.

Brandon helped us move cattle. I liked

riding with him. He carved his initials into my chaps with his Buck knife, then rubbed dirt into them so no one could see. I think he likes me. We talked about the ranch. We were getting close to crunch time, and still no responses to the E-mail. We tried to come up with another plan but couldn't think of anything. "We could always rob a bank," I said. "Good idea," he said, laughing.

Dad sent us on an easy circle together— that's why we had time to talk. We rode through a grove of aspens that were already turning. The light the leaves gave off was lime and gold. Winter was on the way. Brandon would soon be leaving for college in Laramie. The thought made me sad. We could always E-mail each other, and he'd be home often, he said.

We found a lot more cattle than Dad had expected on our circle, and it took us a while to gather them all. When we came down the trail and pushed them into the big meadow, Dad loped around behind the herd and helped move them across the creek and up the hill, counting them through the gate as they passed into the new pasture.

We always raced our horses the last two hundred yards home. Dad took off his hat, hit my horse on the rump, and off we went. My horse started bucking. He had taught me to ignore the usual rule of thumb—"Don't pull up on his head," he'd always say, "because then he'll think there's a contest going on and he'll buck even harder. Just let him go, and pretty soon he'll get bored. And for god's sake, try to stay on!"

I did what he told me to do, and it worked. The horse bucked three times, three nice, sure bucks. I grabbed the saddle horn, held on with my knees, grabbed a little mane, and left the reins loose. When he saw the other horses getting ahead of him, he lost interest in getting me off and just kept running. At the end, Dad and Brandon were neck and neck, but just to make sure we didn't forget who was boss, Dad spurred his horse ahead and won.

Brandon stayed for dinner, and after, I

helped load his gelding. When the gate was closed, he took my hand and said, "Don't be worrying about this ranch. We're going to figure something out."

Late August. I invited the puppy I'd picked as my own onto the bed. He was so small he fit in my hand, but his ears and his paws were enormous. I lay on my back and held him on my chest. He moved slowly up and down with my breathing.

When the sun set that night, it seemed to take forever. As if the way to darkness had grown very long. It descended through smoke from a forest fire and passed behind the clouds of a thunderstorm which were salmon, pink, gray, yellow. Then the sky was torn open by the sound of timpani and night poured in. Black. All black.

Morning. Dad marked the calendar: In ten days we would bring the cattle and sheep off the mountain. The banker would be there to count the animals. The few we had. Dad didn't have to say it: this was the beginning of the end. Everything in me wanted to go silent, but now, whatever happened, I couldn't hide.

S<small>EPTE</small>M<small>BE</small>R *is when*

winter starts to show itself a little at a time. First it creeps into the trees in yellow splashes, then summer's wild thunderstorms go down the drain and new clouds come, all white and thick, bearing snow. The bull elk are starting to spar with other bulls. Soon they'll go into rut, ready for mating. The birds begin flocking and ducks and ducklings do maneuvers, getting ready to fly south to a warmer climate. By the end of the month, even when it is still warm,

there are fall colors in the aspens and cotton-
wood trees.

* * *

Sheep camp means happiness. I was staying in the sheep wagon again, helping Pedro and Fermina bring the sheep off the mountain. Our wagon was parked on a high ridge, 5,000 feet above the valley. We could see the storms blowing in from the northwest where they swept across Montana, then us. The first morning there was ice on the water bucket, and I could see my breath as I split kindling for the woodstove. Pedro was singing as he cooked breakfast: tortillas, ham, cheese, eggs, hot peppers. Fermina and I grained the horses and fed the dog. For a moment I forgot all my sorrows. Nobody would ever find us, nobody could take this from us, could they?

We gathered the sheep and began pushing them down the mountain. Across the stream, through the pine forest, then a long traverse to the far side of the mountain. From there we could see more than a hundred miles. Long strings of trees lined the streams. It was impossible to get lost there. We came across an old log cabin in a thicket of lodgepole pines. The sod roof was caved in, but the walls, made of thick, handhewn logs, were solid. We got off our horses and stepped inside. We found a coffeepot and some old mugs and a pile of badly deteriorated papers inside a tin can with a lid. Could you rebuild the roof? I asked Pedro. He glanced around and nodded. "Maybe so, I think I can."

"Good," I said. He looked at me, puzzled. "This is where we can hide when they come to take the ranch away."

As the sheep started their long march off the mountain, I thought of the day Pedro had come down carrying Fermina. I had been so young then I didn't know what it meant to be a foundling, to be abandoned by your mother, set down somewhere. Now I had an inkling of what that must be like. Even if Fermina had been too young then to remember now—still, somewhere inside, she must know. The moment when she no longer felt herself being held. That's how I felt, too. The ranch's embrace was loosening, and soon I too might be without a home.

After a few hours the sheep strung out into a long thick line with two dogs trotting along behind them. Pedro, Fermina, and I rode three abreast. Nothing and no one could divide us. They could take the sheep, but they couldn't take us away from one other.

We camped another night near a spring. Dad came in the pickup and brought us dinner. He was his usual sarcastic, funny self. He and Pedro talked about the condition of the lambs, how much they'd weigh, how much they'd bring at market. Fermina and I went exploring. The creek was full of trout, so we each cut off a willow branch, tied a fishing line to the end, hung on a hook and a worm, and off we went. Within an hour we supplemented dinner with ten "brookies," which Pedro cooked in the frying pan.

In the morning we took the sheep all the

way to the sorting corrals. There was one semi waiting. Usually there were three or four. But that's all the lambs we had to ship this year. We cut the lambs off from the ewes and loaded them onto the three-tiered truck.

I hadn't noticed before, but Brandon's dad, the banker, was there counting lambs, making notes. Mom sat in the pickup looking fearful. I'd resolved to put all this out of my mind. Fermina and I worked hard, moving the animals through narrow alleyways. If they thought they were afraid, they should have asked us how we felt.

After shipping, Dad made pancakes, bacon, and eggs for all of us in the little cookhouse. It was an old tradition of ours to feed the truckers before their long journey began. I'd just as soon be feeding the lambs, but that wasn't possible. The ewes, suddenly feeling their loss, were noisy. After breakfast, the banker and Dad went outside and talked. I didn't know what they said, but Dad looked kind of bad when he came inside. The trucks backed around and left.

* * *

Morning. Dad insisted that I picket-break my young colt, which means teaching him to graze on a picket chain. That way, we could take him on pack trips or use him at sheep camp. After a few minutes the horse got the idea, throwing his nose in the air to lift the heavy chain so he could move around. When he got to the end of the chain attached to a picket driven into the ground, he stopped, balked a little, stared, then continued eating. "He'll be fine," Dad said, and we rode off to check a fence.

When we got back there was something wrong. The colt was lying down with the chain wrapped around his back leg and there was blood on the grass. His leg was broken.

I knew what came next, and I couldn't watch. Dad was so upset his hands were shaking and tears fell from his eyes. Before Dad could get his gun and load it, I took off down the road, headed off the mountain, away from the sound of my horse dying, away from my father, who was losing everything, away from all humans who were so wrong and so hateful. I ran part of the way. The road was dusty and rutted deeply by summer thunderstorms. I wanted my colt back, I wanted to train him my own way. I'd never listen to my father again.

A pickup rumbled behind me, slowly, getting closer. I didn't look to see who it was. The truck stopped. I heard my name being called. It was my mother. I turned to her. She said, "You better jump on in." She didn't have to ask if anything was wrong. After a long time she asked what had happened and I told her, half-told her, and she said, "Oh, baby, I'm so sorry," and reached across the seat to put her arm around me. I tried not to give in, but then I couldn't hold back, and I buried my head in her shoulder and cried.

The next day the banker came to the house. He had his calculator out at the kitchen table, and when the batteries went dead he cursed; then his face went red, and Dad had to give him one of ours. He wrote a bunch of stuff down on a big piece of yellow legal paper and showed it to Dad, and Dad made some notes and slid the paper back to him, and the banker shook his head. I couldn't really hear all they were saying, but I heard the words *operating costs*, and *debt*, and *upping the numbers*.

I went to the corral and saddled a horse, and as I was trotting off, the banker was leaving. He stuck his head out the window and waved— "Don't worry, maybe something will happen yet"—but I could only glower at him, and kicked my horse and loped away.

I didn't come home until long after dark. I rode up into the mountains and tried to find the broken-down log cabin Pedro, Fermina, and I had stumbled on. But I got lost in the thick timber. There was so much deadfall, it was hard to see, and there was no real trail but lots of bear sign, and dark little rivulets of water, and bogs sodden with fallen pine needles, and the strange, creaking sounds of lodgepole pines knocking about in the wind.

I rode and rode. The deadfall was like giant

pick-up sticks lying all over the place, and my horse had to climb over all the trunks and his feet sometimes got stuck between the limbs, and I had to get off and lift his leg out and go on. I wanted to find that cabin and start shoring up the caved-in roof and make it a place where I could live and hide, even though I'd promised myself I wouldn't hide anymore, but now, with my colt gone, and the banker coming to take everything away, what was the use?

Once I came out of the timber, but found myself on the edge of a vertical cliff that dropped 2,000 feet into the valley north of the ranch, so I had to go back into the trees and try to pick out a trail that would take me back to the road.

Dad was awfully upset when I finally got home, scared that something bad had happened to me. He sent me to my room. There was nothing cooking in the kitchen and I asked where Mom was, and he looked hurt and said she had gone to her sister's, which was a six-hour drive away. It was then that I wished I had a sister, someone to go to, but I had no one, except Pedro and Fermina, and they were at sheep camp.

After a while I went downstairs. Dad was busy at the kitchen table with his calculator and the accounting books and the yellow papers the banker had left with him. We didn't speak. I went to the refrigerator and hacked off a piece of elk roast and got some bread and milk and as I began to go upstairs he said, "I'm sorry . . . about everything." I nodded and took my food upstairs. There was no one in the world who understood and no one to talk to. I held my puppy close, but even he wriggled away.

September 14. Snow. Highway closed. Electricity out. Mother came home and things got back to normal, more or less, though now they were talking about selling our mountain allotment, and some of the spring pastures to make ends meet, which I thought was a bad idea, because even if we had some cattle, where would we take them in the summer to graze if we didn't have our mountain pastures? But who was I to say what we should do?

Mom and I stood out on the porch and watched snowflakes drift down. Soon the grass was covered, and the snow hung in sagebrush like thick cobwebs. I checked my E-mail. Nothing of interest. Brandon called to console me about my colt. He was real sweet on the phone.

Mom said first snow is like first love. It comes unexpectedly and breaks the branches of trees still laden with green leaves. "Is that what happened to you?" I asked, and she nodded her head. I wondered when I would feel that way.

By evening the snow was gone, but the chill remained. Everywhere there were little clots of white in green grass. By the time winter came, would we still be here?

September 15. High thin clouds masked the sun. The morning was cold. Dad and I made chokecherry jam. We stirred the cherries I picked yesterday and watched the mixture thicken, then poured it into Ball jars and let it cool down. By afternoon the day was hot.

Purple asters bloomed outside the outhouse door. A wasp fell on my nose, stinging me, so that in a few hours, my face was half a bubble. How long had the nighthawks been gone? And where did they go? Why wasn't I paying more attention? The preoccupation with losing the ranch made me lose it before it was gone. School had begun, but I skipped afternoon sports to come home early and help with chores. Apples were ripe. I picked gunnysacks full of them, and Mom and I made apple jelly on the cookstove. When I looked at her questioningly, she shook her head no. Don't ask why we're doing this, the look said. Then she said coolly, "We can take this with us, at least." We began laughing at the absurdity of it all.

September 21. Fall equinox. The equinoxes and solstices are supposed to be times of balance and equipoise. I stood on one foot and tried to balance without wiggling, then attempted to get an egg to stand on its pointed end and succeeded.

I remembered something from a poem we

read in school: "The end is the beginning." But what did it mean? I'd seen life come out of death on the ranch, but when banks got involved, I didn't see anything happening that didn't go their way. Banks had nothing to do with living and dying in a real sense—banks didn't breathe.

After breakfast and before school, I took the puppies for a walk to the waterfall. Far above the ranch I heard an elk bugle: it was a high-pitched whistle that rose up then swooped down and ended in a low, three-part grunt. He was in rut, guarding his harem and letting other bulls know this was his territory. As the light in the sky decreased, the light in the berry bushes and trees got brighter and brighter. Meadowlarks began to flock. Mallards practiced flying in Vs, taking off and landing on the pond. The smell of pine had been replaced with the smell of snow.

NINE

OCTOBER is the month when we begin preparing for winter. Ten cords of firewood are cut and stacked, headgates are shut off and greased, tarp dams rolled up and put away, horses' shoes taken off, saddle blankets washed, saddles and bridles saddle-soaped, and the last of the garden produce is harvested, blanched, then frozen. Up in the mountains, grizzly and black bears begin searching for a den or fixing up an old one. Beaver cut willow branches for their winter food, and the last of the *birds congregate. Starlings wheel over the corn-fields in the valley, spinning silver then black. The light changes, yellowing with the cotton-wood leaves. Mule deer and pronghorn antelope are in rut, bald eagles hunker down on fence posts, the weasel changes its summer coat from brown to one that is white as snow.*

* * *

October 7. Fourteen degrees this morning with a skiff of snow on the ground. Long icicles hung from the eaves like teeth, so I could imagine I'd been eaten by a whale, like Jonah. Then one broke and the pieces caught in a cobweb: a spearpoint and a comma. Lake ice began to look like the map of a brain, and the bare hill above the house turned maroon and burnt umber, frosted over with snow. Later, hot sun jumped off snow and struck my face. My lips peeled. I rode the back pasture high above the ranch near the waterfall. Up top, I picked gooseberries, filling my saddlebags with them.

On the way down the mountain I saw three

semis pulling into the ranch yard below, then the brand inspector. I froze in place. Could it be the bankers taking our animals away? I trotted fast down the mountain. A driver and two women got out of the cab as I approached.

"Hi. I'm Betty and this is Ursula. Are you Timmy?" They were smiling, but it was all happening so fast I couldn't understand who they were or what they were doing. They asked me to get my parents. I ran into the house and yelled. Mother called Dad, who was in the shed fixing the tractor. We got back out and the women introduced themselves all over again. Betty began:

"We got a copy of your daughter's E-mail. It was very moving, very courageous of her to write it."

My parents looked at me askance, but the woman continued. "We were so impressed we thought, by god, we better do something."

"Wait a minute, what E-mail? What did it say?" Dad asked.

Betty and Ursula looked at each other, then

smiled at me and continued with their story. "So we've gone around to different ranchers in our area and asked them if they could donate an animal or two, maybe an older cow with a calf, or anything that was healthy." She motioned to the loaded semi. "I'm sorry these cattle aren't too fancy, but they do have calves at their sides and they're not so used up that they won't breed back."

Dad peered into the slats of the truck: it was full of cattle. He looked at me, astonished.

Ursula chimed in: "We're hoping that your banker will accept these as collateral and give you another year to rebuild your herd. We sure hope these extra cattle will help."

My father looked from the two women to me, then Mother, and back again, absolutely stunned. I stepped forward to shake hands with the women and thank them, but when I saw my mother's face—tears streaming down her cheeks—something happened to me. All the fears rose up to the surface. I put my hand over my mouth, then the tears came.

"Well, I'll be go to hell," my father said. That cracked us all up, and the crying turned to laughter. Then, before I knew it, the two women were hugging me and my mother and were shaking hands with my father. Even the crusty old brand inspector turned away so we couldn't see his face. Then he and the driver and my father commenced to unload the cattle.

Morning. We cut the calves off from their mothers and let them settle for a few days. Dad and I turned them out into a fresh pasture with plenty of feed and water and moved the mother cows down with the others, turning them out onto fall range.

Dad hadn't said too much. He was still in a state of shock. But when we were alone together he finally asked, "When did you do this, and where did you get this idea?"

I told him that it happened on the Fourth of July up at cow camp, that it wasn't just me, but all the kids, especially Brandon. "You told me to always go to the source for ideas, so I did. I didn't want to tell you about it. I didn't think you'd approve. But I had to do something. I felt so useless."

We crossed a creek and let the horses drink. It was a warm day—Indian summer. I looked at Dad. "Anyway, when you love something a lot, you have to try to save its life—whether it's a ranch or a person or a dog or a calf—at least, that's what you always taught me."

Dad stared at me. He tried to say something, but only his mouth moved. I began to smile. He blew his nose, which scared his colt. When she jumped, he almost fell off. I laughed so hard my eyes got wet. "You are really something else, Sunshine," he said, then thumped my gelding on his rump and together, we loped up the hill.

On the way home we took a detour to the ruins of the homesteader's cabin. The foundations of his stone house were still there. I rode under an apple tree and picked apples—one for me, one for my horse. Stepping off and slipping the bridle from his head, I fed him half an apple, then the other half. We picked wild asparagus that grew along the bank of the irrigation ditch and was kept fresh all summer by the passing water. A fragrance wafted by; I looked up— Dad was holding a bunch of iris, blue, dark purple, yellow, and red—flowers the homesteader planted eighty years ago. Doffing his hat, Dad handed them to me. "Thank you," he said. That's all he said. I pressed the petals from those flowers into my journal.

Why was the world fading when I'd just discovered joy? Why had the songbirds gone? Why was the lake empty of ducks, why were the deer migrating down, why were the brown trout only now spawning, why did the bull elk echo their urgent whistling calls against rock walls? Why did the forest's understory turn red? Why did the streams freeze at night and thaw in the morning? Why, in the midst of happiness, did I sometimes feel sad, as if the close call of almost losing our ranch had changed me, stirred something up in my heart I didn't know about before?

N OVEMBER *is the month when animals go into hibernation or become dormant for short periods of time. That's how I feel, too. Blustery storms give way to a permanent lacquer of snow. Bears go into their dens and sleep on soft beds of pine boughs. Hawks come down out of the mountains to hunt mice and voles, and elk follow the rivers into the valleys to winter range. Sage grouse migrate south—all life draining down out of the*

high country—and we are left with magpies,
ravens, eagles, and hawks, and long days and
nights of near-silence, except for the creaking of
snow under our feet.

✳ ✳ ✳

November 1. Dad, Mom, and I plus a couple of
friends—cowboys from Montana who were
passing through—gathered our new, larger herd
of cattle and began bringing them home out of
the hills, what we call fall range. Saddling up at
4:30 A.M., we rode out in the dark at a fast trot.
The moon was a sliver, and a fat wedge of cold
wind blew off the ridges. We were all dressed in
long underwear, jeans, chaps, Scotch caps, and
gloves. Because we couldn't see very well, we
rode with a loose rein and let the horse pick the
way, zigzagging around sagebrush like slalom
racers.

Since our cattle came Dad had been in high
spirits. He shoved the fried egg sandwich Mom
made into my pocket. Only thing was, the yolk
wasn't hard, and it turned into a gooey mess

leaking down my chaps. Later he rode alongside me, slipped off my horse's bridle, and whopped my horse on the rump to make him go. Go we did, but only a few yards. We all laughed so hard that one guy's horse started bucking, and off he went. When I asked him later what happened, he grinned and said, "I was on the north end of a southbound horse, is all."

It was evening by the time we reached the final stretch home. We brought "the gather"— the cattle—back through the hills, then along the highway in the dark. It was hard for passing cars to see us and we took it slowly, because the new cows didn't know the way. One neighbor stopped and passed us a thermos cup of coffee. My hands were so cold, I couldn't tell if I was holding the cup or not, but it tasted good.

That night snow fell, with another six inches due. "Just a skiff," they keep saying, but even skiffs add up to something. By morning the snow had stopped but an icy mist had fallen over the rolling hills, shrouding thickets of wild plum trees. Later the sun came out and grasshoppers jumped, for a moment lifting summer back into play. It felt good to have at least a handful of cattle.

Mid-November. More than a foot of snow fell, and the temperature dropped below zero. Our big pond froze over. Ducks were gone. I didn't have a chance to say farewell. Mist swallowed the whole ranch and crawled up the red rock walls. Icicles hung from roofs, then dropped down like knives. If you could cut open the earth deeply enough, what would you see? I dreamt it was gray with fog inside the house, and we got lost trying to find the bathroom. Coyotes howled.

After school, I followed a deer's track across the frozen pond and came back the other way tracking my dog, Rusty. His prints looked like music: a print, a drag mark, another print. Walking, I pushed snow in front of my feet into mounds of glitter. At noon on Saturday it was six degrees below zero. That was how the end began and in that way, the end became a beginning. It happened when all else on the planet was dying. When the fruit had withered and the birds were flying south, and the world grew hushed and there was almost nothing to do. We took afternoon naps even if we didn't need them, and the horses were turned out to rest and the haying equipment was parked inside the barn and Brandon's dad didn't have to bother us anymore. At least, not this year.

We took turns building fires in the morning and splitting kindling just the right size for the cookstove. Our entire house was heated with woodstoves—one in every room. We ate soup and stew and bread, pies and cakes from the oven. I taught the puppies to lie down, sit, stay, go way around, come back, to jump, turn left and right, and they taught me to relax with things as they are and to play. I read and read and read—all the books I had piled up all spring and summer—and some evenings we listened to music—classical, Indian, African, Cuban— you name it. It was like traveling without having to move. I felt so grateful just to be where we were.

Two days before Thanksgiving we took food to the herders all over the county. Not just Pedro, but the herders who worked for other ranchers, too. I didn't know why. It was just what we did.

"You got some of that owl meat for me?" old Jack asked as we lifted a big pan of turkey into his wagon. "Must be November, then," he said. "To tell the truth, I'd kinda lost count a while back." When he said a while back, he probably meant about fifty years ago.

Then there was Bob, who liked to shoot at cattle to keep them from stealing the sheep's feed, and John, who had a metal plate in his head and had been struck by lightning three times and never knew where he was. He said the sheep showed him the way up and down the mountain and he didn't need to go anywhere else. Rudy owned a Cadillac convertible that he kept in town, but owned nothing else except the clothes he had on. There was

Sterling, who tried to shoot himself once but missed, so Dad just put blanks in his gun and Sterling didn't know the difference, or if he did, he didn't mention it. Pancho, who'd had his ear bitten off in a bar fight and sent money home to his wife, who spent it on her lover and the children they'd had together—how would Pancho know, he hadn't been home for eighteen years. Pancho was like St. Francis, and made crosses for every dead bird, horse, lamb, bee, marmot, or snake he saw. Dad said that one year, after an early snowstorm, the forest was littered with crosses: "It was eerie, like the whole world was a graveyard."

Besides turkey, we made a pie for each man and a bowl of dressing and gave him a bag of new potatoes, and some candy, and a six-pack of beer.

On Thanksgiving Day we began cooking before dawn. Later, Pedro and Fermina joined us for dinner. We ate wild foods: duck and pheasant and Hungarian partridge; venison and elk; lamb's quarters, puffball mushrooms, rosehip jam, wild plum pudding, and wine the neighbor had made. This year, we didn't slide over the thanks—we went around the table and each of us talked a little about how hard the year had been and how the kindness of strangers, as well as neighbors, had saved our ranch. Pedro gave a blessing in Spanish, I wanted to cry again, this time with happiness, but I didn't. The food was passed, and we ate slowly and with gusto.

D<small>ECEMBER</small> *is the month when the sun disappears and all the light seems to emanate from the ground as if snow were a single lamp smeared over the globe. But why are some lights cold and others hot? December 1 slides into December 10, which veers down a narrow tunnel toward the winter solstice. Darkness keeps coming, and we fight against it by lighting candles everywhere. Instead of riding horses we travel on skis. The pregnant cows are brought in closer to the house.*

Every morning we feed them with a team of horses and a wagon. It takes half an hour to hitch up, but what's the hurry, it's our biggest chore of the day.

✻ ✻ ✻

December 18. Dad put sleigh bells on the harness. That's how he celebrated the season. He pretended he was gruff, but he really wasn't at all. When school was out, we all rode along and helped stack hay and peel off flakes like slices of bread as the wagon bumped along. If it wasn't too cold, we stopped by the frozen creek to drink tea and coffee from thermoses. The puppies were big enough to ride on the wagon with us. Some we'd given away, but we kept three.

December 21. Winter solstice. The shortest day of the year. We'd barely finished feeding the cattle when it got dark. This is my least favorite day of the year. I made a big black mark on the calendar and pouted a little bit, but Dad kept encouraging me to see it another way: the next day spring began, he told me, as it was only going to get lighter from then on.

Christmas Eve. Despite all the romantic pictures of men on horseback bringing a Christmas tree home to a lonely log cabin, it just wasn't practical. First of all, the snow was deep and hardpacked by wind, and the horses would have to be sharpshod because it was so slippery. Instead, we put on skis and did a herringbone walk up the mountain to the forest. We decided to pick a little tree—nothing too ostentatious, Mother said, to go along with the leanness of the year. There were to be no presents bought in town, only things we'd made for each other.

The tree was the top of a lodgepole pine that had snapped off during a windstorm. Dad laid it on a big piece of cardboard tied to a rope around his waist, and in this way skidded the tree home behind him. At home, we decorated the tree with a single strand of white lights—nothing else, but with almost daylong darkness, it cheered the room.

Christmas morning. Dad left early and brought Pedro and Fermina into the ranch from sheep camp. Pedro was carrying presents: a pair of braided rawhide reins he made for each of us. Fermina had whittled a whole menagerie of animals and birds out of tiny pine and willow sticks. Some were imaginary: animals that were half horses, half human, dogs with antlers, elk with fish for hands, bears with long braided hair coming off their heads. Mom had made food for everyone—boxes and boxes of cookies, ginger cakes, brownies, fruit cakes soaked in rum, and chocolate truffles. Dad made elkhide chaps for each of us with lovely fringe on the sides and silver conchos he'd saved from his father's chaps to decorate the legs. And what did I make? Well, not much, I'm afraid. I wrote this, a diary of the year—not only an account of our hardships, but also a kind of almanac of the seasons. To go with it, I did some watercolors and drawings, then had the whole booklet copied and gave one to each member of the family. In

Pedro's, I wrote an introduction in Spanish, something he could read by himself. It seemed that everyone, in their way, had given so much. Maybe that was what the Indian giveaway was all about. It didn't just mean giving away your horse and blanket. It was a state of mind, like riding a horse that is bucking. We all learned to "turn loose" this year.

After dinner we all went skating on the pond. Dad started a little fire off to one side where we could warm our hands. Pedro had never tried skating before and Dad lent him his skates. Fermina was a real pro, and she held one of Pedro's arms and I held the other as he wobbled out onto the ice. Mom played a waltz on the pickup's tape deck. Soon enough, Pedro got the hang of it and burst forward, arms outstretched, and made a long, graceful glide to the left before crashing.

New Year's Eve. Now it was about to begin again. The ending, that is. Or was it a beginning that was ending? I couldn't keep track anymore.

When I felt panicky about what might happen to us—the ranch, our animals, our whole extended family—I just watched the young dogs. In their moment-to-moment life they breathed, played, slept, scratched, ate, drank, chased cattle. They were purely themselves and loved one another and us unconditionally, just the way they lived.

Friends came over, among them Brandon and his parents. We thanked them quietly for all they had done—or not done, in the case of Brandon's dad. At midnight, everyone kissed, then the dancing began.

JaNuaRY is the snow-covered month, the month that makes you gasp from cold. It puts out your eyes with darkness, and puts them back in again with the northern lights. The month, like the aurora, is the still point in a year that is always moving. Under the ground all kinds of animals are sleeping—squirrels, snakes, voles, mice, marmots, etc. Sometimes they wake up for a few hours and eat or move around, then they go back to sleep. Their subterranean homes and roadways are elaborate.

Some are lined with grass hay; bears' beds are lined with pine boughs. When I wander around in winter I think about what's under my feet: prairie dog towns and vole chambers . . . all those sleepy lives under the quick thunder of my skis.

* * *

January 8. Today we had seven inches of snow in seven hours. It twisted as it fell, stirred by some invisible hand: there was no wind. When I skied up the mountain, my tracks were covered with white as soon as they were made. Snow fell through leafless trees. That looked like sad men with outstretched arms. Stands of rock were flesh-colored. Ice covered the creeks. I put my ear down and heard the faint tinkling of water. Red algae grew in snow-banks on the upper slopes—at least there was some life. Under a giant sage bush I saw the matted grass where two deer slept last night. A double bed. Now the deer had gone down to the valley to browse. Only snow moved. And a magpie squawking as I passed under her tree.

I climbed to the upper field, through barbed wire, onto the steep slope behind the ranch. The snow was dry and soft and powdery. It flew from my legs like feathers. I followed one set of tracks, then another. Small and large, walking, running, and jumping. Yet when I looked around, there was nothing there. Smoke curled from the ranch house chimney far below, and a raven ahead of me cawed, as if saying, "Come on . . . there's no going back, follow me." I kept trudging. A thin crust of snow formed on top of powder—like hard candy—which I broke with my skis and knees. Breath, crunch, breath, crunch, squeak, exhale.

Sometimes, in a dark moment, I wonder if it might not all have fallen apart—the ranch, my parents', Pedro's, and Fermina's lives. How close did we come? What kept it from happening? Part of the answer is that each of us acted—we tried to do something to help in our own way. We learned that it does no good to give up, even if you are stymied for a while, you just keep working at holding it together. We gave each other some room to be angry and sad without blame, without shame. We all cried openly many times. Now, when something else goes very wrong, we will know better how to see it, and how to find a solution. We'll know that soon the pain we're in will pass, and none of us will die from it. Just like that celebrated day of almost no light, which carried inside its brevity the promise of spring.